THE THREE PRINCES

THE THREE PRINCES

A Tale from the Middle East

retold by Eric A. Kimmel

illustrated by Leonard Everett Fisher

Holiday House/New York

Notes About the Book

The story of "The Three Princes" is known throughout the Middle East. I first heard it in 1983, when I was teaching a class in storytelling at Portland State University. Several of my students were from Saudi Arabia. "The Three Princes" was one of many wonderful stories they shared with me. Since then, I have come across Egyptian, Moroccan, and Persian versions of the tale. It also appears in later editions of the collection of stories known as *The Arabian Nights*.

—E.A.K.

During World War II, I served with the U.S. Army Corps of Engineers in Morocco and Algeria. I became intrigued with the Muslim culture I found there. Illustrating "The Three Princes" provided me with an opportunity to recreate the essence of the Arab world.

I prepared the art by painting illustration boards black, then drawing my designs on them with white chalk. The chalk drawings and black under-painting disappeared beneath a final application of acrylic color.

—L.E.F.

To Doris Kimmel—wise as well as beautiful

E.A.K.

To Margery Fisher—beautiful as well as wise

L.E.F.

Text copyright © 1994 by Eric A. Kimmel
Illustrations copyright © 1994 by Leonard Everett Fisher
Printed in the United States of America
All rights reserved

Library of Congress Cataloging-in-Publication Data
Kimmel, Eric A.
The three princes : a tale from the Middle East / retold by Eric
A. Kimmel ; illustrated by Leonard Everett Fisher. — 1st ed.
p.   cm.
Summary: A princess promises to marry the prince who finds the
most precious treasure.
ISBN 0-8234-1115-X
[1. Fairy tales.   2. Folklore, Arab.]   I. Fisher, Leonard
Everett, ill.   II. Three princes.   III. Title.
PZ8.K527Tf   1994   93-25862   CIP   AC
398.21—dc20
[E]
ISBN 0-8234-1553-8 (pbk.)

This story first appeared in *Cricket, The Magazine for Children*

Once there was and once there was not a princess who was as wise as she was beautiful. Princes from all over the world sought her hand in marriage, but the ones she liked best were three cousins: Prince Fahad, Prince Muhammed, and Prince Mohsen.

Prince Fahad and Prince Muhammed were men of wealth and renown, although they were neither young nor handsome. Prince Mohsen, by contrast, was tall and slender as a reed. His flashing eyes melted the princess's heart the first time she saw him. However, as the youngest son of a poor king, Prince Mohsen possessed little more than his handsome face, his cloak, and his camel. Nonetheless, he was the one the princess loved and the one she was determined to marry.

The wazir, her chief minister, scoffed at her decision. "Mohsen? He has nothing to give you."

"Then I will give him a chance to find something," the princess said. Summoning the three princes, she said to them, "Go out into the world for a year and bring back the rarest thing you find in your travels. I will marry the prince who returns with the greatest wonder."

The next morning the three princes rode out together. They traveled across the desert for many days until they came to a place where the path branched off in three directions.

"This is a sign that we should separate," Prince Fahad said.

Prince Muhammed and Prince Mohsen agreed. Prince Fahad took the path to the right, Prince Muhammed took the path to the left, and Prince Mohsen continued straight on across the desert.

After one year's time they returned to the place where the three paths met. They camped for the night, sharing stories of their adventures. One by one the stars came out.

"What great wonder did you find on your travels?" Prince Fahad asked Prince Muhammed.

Prince Muhammed replied, "I traveled across the Iron Mountains to the distant Hadramaut. In a cave guarded by a frightful djinn, I found a great wonder." He reached under his cloak and took out a crystal ball.

"A crystal ball? What is so wonderful about that?" his cousins asked.

"This is no ordinary crystal ball," Prince Muhammed replied. "When I peer inside it, I can see what is happening anywhere in the world. Is that not a wonderful thing?"

His cousins agreed that it was.

Prince Muhammed turned to Prince Fahad. "What wonder did you bring back from your travels?"

Prince Fahad answered, "I traveled across Egypt's desert sands. In the tomb of a forgotten king, I discovered this." He unwrapped a bundle and spread it on the ground. It was a carpet.

"A carpet? What is so wonderful about that?" Prince Muhammed and Prince Mohsen asked him.

Prince Fahad replied, "This is a flying carpet. It can carry me wherever I want to go in less time than it takes to tell about it. Is that not a wonderful thing?"

His cousins agreed that it was.

Then Prince Fahad and Prince Muhammed turned to Prince Mohsen. "What rare and wonderful thing did you find on your travels?" they asked.

"I journeyed to the shores of the Great Sea," Prince Mohsen replied. "There I met a sailor who gave me this!" He opened his hand and held out an orange.

His cousins began to laugh. "Is that all? An ordinary orange?"

"This is not an ordinary orange!" Prince Mohsen protested. "It is a healing orange. It can cure any illness, even if a person is dying."

"If what you say is true, then this orange is the greatest wonder of all," the other two princes said. However, they did not sound as if they really believed it.

As the three princes sat under the starry sky, Prince Mohsen happened to remark, "I wonder if the princess is well. We have not seen her in a year."

"Gather around," Prince Muhammed said. "My crystal ball can show her to us." The three princes peered inside the crystal ball together.

A tragic scene appeared before their eyes. There lay the princess, pale as death. The wazir and the ladies and gentlemen of her court stood around her bed, weeping. Doctors bent over her, shaking their heads. The princes lowered their ears to the crystal ball and found they could hear what the doctors were saying. "Our princess is dying. She will not live to see the sun rise."

"The princess needn't die. My orange can cure her," Prince Mohsen cried. "But how can I reach her in time? Even if I rode all night, I could never arrive by morning."

"My carpet can carry us there in an instant," Prince Fahad said. "Quick, get on!"

The three princes leaped onto the flying carpet. In less time than it takes to tell about it, the carpet whisked them through the air all the way to the princess's palace. The princes ran through the gates, crying, "Clear the way! Let us through!" Crowds of courtiers parted to let them pass.

Prince Mohsen knelt beside the dying princess. He cut the healing orange into four pieces. As soon as the princess tasted the first piece, her color returned. The second piece, and her eyes opened. The third, and she sat up in bed. By the time she finished the last piece, she was completely cured.

"A miracle!" the wazir cried. The courtiers echoed, "A miracle!"

"It is a miracle indeed," the princess said. "These three noble princes have restored me to life. I will marry the prince who was most responsible for saving me."

"Which one is that?" everyone asked.

"The princess obviously means Prince Mohsen, for it was his orange that cured her," the doctors said.

"True," the courtiers replied. "But the orange had to arrive in time to be of any use. Prince Fahad's magic carpet brought it here, so he is the one who really saved her."

"But neither the orange nor the carpet would have done any good if the princes had not known that the princess was dying," the wazir pointed out. "I say it was Prince Muhammed's crystal ball that was most responsible for restoring our princess to life."

The doctors and the courtiers and the wazir argued and argued, but could not agree. So in the end they did what they should have done in the beginning. They asked the princess.

"Which prince truly saved your life? Which one are you going to marry?"

The princess answered, "No prince could have saved me by himself. Each needed the help of his companions. All three played an equal part, and I am grateful to them all."

"But you cannot marry them all!" the wazir protested.

"I know. I must choose one . . . and the one I choose is—Prince Mohsen!"

"Mohsen? Why not Muhammed? Why not Fahad?" everyone asked.

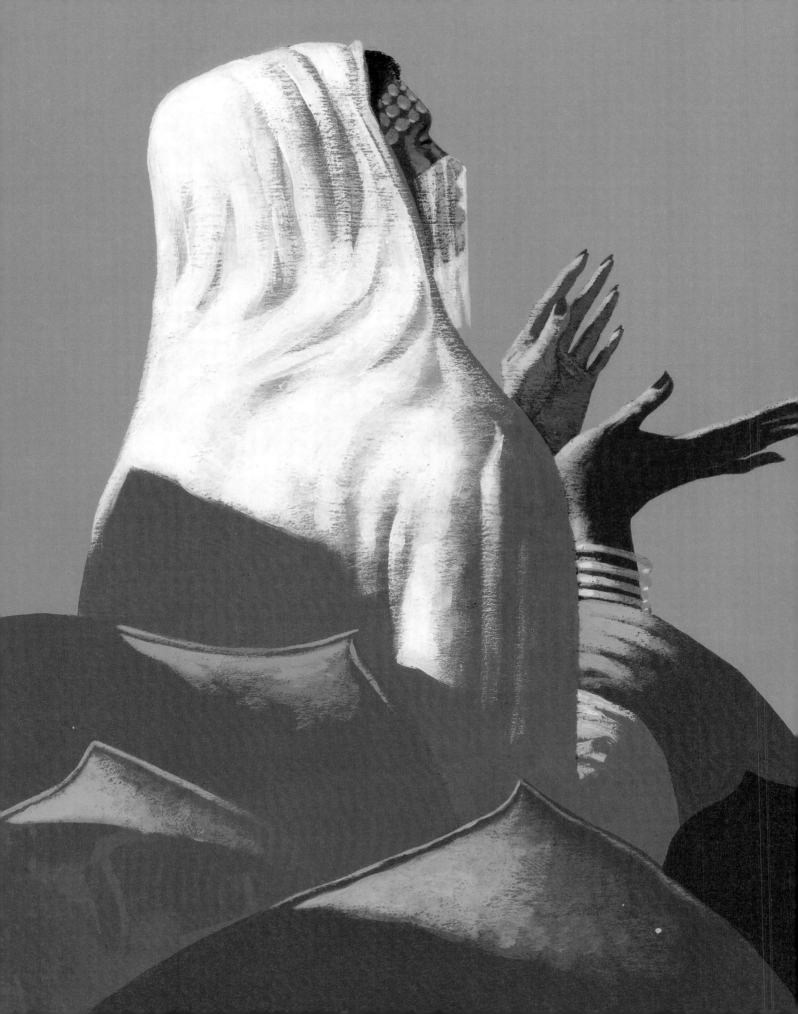